Twilight Sparkle ✶✶ and ✶✶ The Crystal Heart Spell

Written by G. M. Berrow

Little, Brown and Company
New York ✶ Boston

Little, Brown and Company

Hachette Book Group
1290 Avenue of the Americas, New York, NY 10104
Visit our website at www.lb-kids.com

Little, Brown and Company is a division of Hachette Book Group, Inc.
The Little, Brown name and logo are trademarks of Hachette Book Group, Inc.

The publisher is not responsible for websites (or their content) that are not owned by the publisher.

First Edition: April 2013

Library of Congress Cataloging-in-Publication Data

Berrow, G. M.
   Twilight Sparkle and the Crystal Heart Spell / written by G.M. Berrow.—1st ed.
      p. cm.—(My little pony)
   Summary: "Twilight Sparkle, a very special pony and a loyal apprentice of Princess Celestia, sets off on an adventure to find the Crystal Heart Spell and learn to be a true leader"—Provided by publisher.
   ISBN 978-0-316-22819-0
   I. Title.
PZ7.B4615Twi 2013
[Fic]—dc23

2012040521

10 9

RRD-C

Printed in the United States of America

For my three "mane" girls—
Rachel, Pam, and Sidnie

CONTENTS

* * *

CHAPTER 1
A Crown Achievement 1

CHAPTER 2
A Foal House 13

CHAPTER 3
Empire State of Mind 25

CHAPTER 4
A Tail to Tell 33

CHAPTER 5
A Gift Horse 49

CHAPTER 6
On a Scroll 59

CHAPTER 7
Brainstorming the Castle 73

CHAPTER 8
Gilda's Got Game 79

CHAPTER 9
A Head in the Clouds 89

CHAPTER 10
Drinking the Lily Pad Slime 95

CHAPTER 11
Rallying the Hoofs 107

CHAPTER 12
Crystal Clear 113

CHAPTER 13
PFF to the Rescue 121

A Special Surprise 135

CHAPTER 1

A Crown
Achievement

★ ★ ★

All of Equestria had been celebrating since
the joyous wedding of Shining Armor and
Princess Mi Amore Cadenza. Cadance, as
she was called, was one of the most loving
mares in all of ponydom. The citizens of
Equestria, including the newly recovered
Crystal Empire, were living in a time of

happiness and prosperity. Apples grew in the orchards, creatures big and small played in the lush green fields, and ponies of all three tribes lived in harmony. And now, another promising young royal had been inducted into the highest ranks of pony society. It seemed like the cherry on top of a delicious ice-cream sundae.

Ponies of all kinds from the far reaches of Princess Celestia's kingdom were curious about the new princess who had just been crowned. She wasn't just anypony. This was a young Unicorn pony with a violet-hued hide, a beautiful purple-and-pink-striped mane, and incredible raw abilities. Her name was Twilight Sparkle, and she was indeed very special. Stories of her amazing magical gifts had even been passed along all the way from San Franciscolt to Manehattan. These tales had started to become legendary—especially the one about the time she took on the formidable ursa minor on her own, or better yet, the time she defeated the evil Queen Chrysalis in order to save the royal court of Canterlot. Everypony was excited to see what wonders would accompany such a unique princess's reign.

Twilight was excited, too. Not only did she bear an esteemed new title, but she had earned something unique as well. Twilight had received her very own set of wings. *Real* Pegasus wings! She was officially a part of a special breed of pony called an Alicorn. This meant that Twilight was now able to harness the magical powers of the Unicorns, the flight abilities of the Pegasi, and the strength of a good, true heart of an Earth

Pony. She was becoming more like her mentor, the talented and kind Princess Celestia, every day.

Although it was very exciting for Twilight to become an Alicorn, she didn't take her new gifts for granted. It was an honor to become part of something so rare and exclusive. She didn't care about all the shiny jewels and castle quarters she'd been given as part of the job. Twilight was happy to remain in Ponyville for now. She loved to spend time studying in her library with Spike, the baby dragon who was her number-one assistant, and having barrels of fun with her best friends. Luxurious castle furnishings could wait.

Ever since Princess Celestia had sent Twilight away from Canterlot to study and learn the magic of friendship, she had really felt that Ponyville was her true home. Twilight was uncertain how she would feel if she had to leave it. And ruling her own kingdom? That was another story.

It was true that Twilight Sparkle loved to help other ponies, to teach them the interesting facts she'd read about in the pages of her beloved books. She also enjoyed her position as designated leader of the Ponyville Winter Wrap-Up. But being in charge of the well-being of a kingdom of ponies didn't seem easy. She could tell that much from having studied with Celestia for all this time. Twilight was nervous. She still had so much to learn about being a leader. But, then again, there was *always* more to learn. Twilight never seemed to be able to acquire enough knowledge on any subject. The world was so vast and fascinating!

★ ✦ ★

One afternoon in Ponyville, just after the Pegasi had moved some clouds into the sky for a short rainfall, Twilight went home to scour every book in her library yet again. She was hoping for some guidance on exactly how a pony could become a great princess and leader. There was bound to be some information that could help a pony out. She thought she was on to something when she first laid a hoof on the pages of *The Princess Bridle*. It was one of her favorite stories about royal ponies, but not quite right.

"What about this one, Twi?" Spike exclaimed, pulling a dusty book with a teal cover from one of the low shelves. He couldn't reach the higher ones without a ladder. Twilight perused the book, titled *Purple Reign* by somepony named Crystal Ball. But that was no good, either. It just had a ton of song lyrics in it.

"Spike!" Twilight exclaimed. "What am I going to do?" She threw her hoof up into the air, exasperated. "I need somepony's help. I just know there's more to being a leader than what I already know." Twilight began to pace around and around the room in her usual manner. She did this so often that the floorboards had worn down, forming a large circle. Spike liked to call it the Twilight Zone.

Spike furrowed his scaly brow and clapped his claws together. "That's it!" He sprang up and knocked several titles from the shelf. A moment later, he appeared in the pile of fallen books clutching one with a familiar blue-and-yellow cover. Twilight recognized it immediately as *Daring Do and the Trek to the Terrifying Tower.* She had already read all the books in the series about the fearless pony adventurer at least three times. Twilight cocked her head to the side. "I don't get it, Spike. What's Daring Do got to 'do' with it?"

"Well, you know how Daring has to rescue a pony who's been locked in a tower surrounded by a moat filled with sharp-toothed piranhas?"

"Yeah...so?"

"And you know how she has to dive into the water in order to get to the tower even though fish are secretly her biggest fear?"

"Spike! Spit it out, already!" Twilight exclaimed. "Do you have an idea on how to help me or not?" She was beginning to look a bit stressed. Her mane had gone frizzy and one of her eyes was twitching ever so slightly. Twilight took her responsibilities very seriously—sometimes too seriously.

"Well, basically Daring Do wants to overcome her fears once and for all. So she asks some older ex-adventurer ponies, like Professor A. B. Ravenhoof, for tips on how to do it!" Spike spread his short arms wide in triumph.

Aha! It was so obvious to Twilight now. She needed guidance. *Real* guidance from somepony who had been around the stable block a few times. "Why didn't *I* think of that?" Twilight's face lit up, thinking of all the ponies she could interview. "Good work, Spike! It's perfect." Spike blushed. He loved nothing more than to be a good assistant to his best friend. But he could hardly say "You're welcome!" before Twilight Sparkle was out the door to find out about the great leaders of Equestria—straight from the horses' mouths.

A Foal House

* * *

"Who in Ponyville might be able to help me?" Twilight said aloud as she trotted through the town square. Then she caught sight of Mayor Mare walking on the opposite side of the courtyard, heading into the town hall with a group of important-looking ponies. The mayor would be a good choice.

She ran their whole town! She would definitely know a thing or two about leadership. It was a good place to start.

But by the time she reached the steps of the town hall, the mayor was already behind closed doors. "Sorry, Princess Twilight," Senior Mint, the tall green guard pony said. "Ms. Mayor Mare is in an important meeting about next year's Summer Sun Celebration and won't be out for some time."

Twilight slumped in defeat. "Oh well. That's all right! But you don't have to call me, um, Princess. Just Twilight will do," she advised. Senior Mint nodded, embarrassed.

"Will you tell her I stopped by?" Twilight asked. Maybe they could talk about being a leader later.

"Yes, of course, Princess Twilight." He

cupped a hoof over his mouth. "Oops, I mean *Just Twilight*." He was clearly a bit nervous around her.

"Thanks!" She flashed her shiny white smile, turned on her hoof, and headed back to square one—wandering around the town square trying to come up with her next move. Suddenly, she smelled the scent of something sweet and scrumptious. Her tummy rumbled in response.

"Fresh cupcakes! Extra icing!" shouted Carrot Cake, the town baker. He pulled a pink-and-yellow cart filled with sugary delicacies of every flavor and color. Maybe it was time for a snack!

"Hello, Mr. Cake!" Twilight said, trotting up to the cart, which had begun to draw a sizable crowd of hungry ponies hoping to snag one of the fragrant delights. Twilight hadn't seen such a commotion since the last cider sale at Sweet Apple Acres.

Mr. Cake nodded in response. "Hiya there, Twilight Sparkle!"

"Is this your new treat cart?" she asked. "What a wonderful idea!"

"Mrs. Cake and I are always trying to come up with new ways to share our desserts with the ponies of Ponyville." Pumpkin Cake and Pound Cake, twin foals, giggled and trotted alongside their father. Pound Cake, who was a Pegasus, beat his little wings until he was hovering near a tray of pink and purple pastries. When his father wasn't watching, he sneakily snatched one and ate it in a single greedy bite. His sister, Pumpkin Cake, jumped as high as she could to grab one, but she couldn't quite reach. She finally used her Unicorn magic to steal a blue cup-cake and deliver it gently to her mouth. She licked her lips with a satisfied smile. Then she burped.

"Plus, the babies love to get out of the shop," Mr. Cake continued, oblivious to his little foals' devious actions. He was too busy dishing out baked goods to the crowd of hungry townsponies. "Fresh air sure does them good!"

Twilight watched as Pumpkin and Pound chased each other. They ran in circles and through the legs of a nearby gray Pegasus pony. The pony wobbled helplessly before toppling over into a nearby rosebush. When she popped her head out, her lemon-yellow mane was adorned with prickly thorns. "Mr. Cake! Do you have any muffins today?" she called as she tried to climb out. Her hoof got caught on a branch, and she tumbled onto the soft grass.

"Fresh out of muffins, unfortunately," Carrot replied, looking concerned.

"Well, *I'll* take one cupcake please." Twilight licked her lips in anticipation. Mr. Cake reached inside the glass display case, but all that was left were crumbs. "Oh dear, we seem to be out of *everything*!" He frowned. His business venture was more successful than he'd expected.

"Why don't you trot back to SugarCube Corner with us?" Carrot offered. "Mrs. Cake is sure to have whipped up some more by now."

Twilight hesitated. She was supposed to be on a fact-finding mission, not lounging around Ponyville eating sweets. Her stomach rumbled again and Pumpkin Cake giggled.

"I guess that's my answer," Twilight said ruefully. "Just for a few minutes, though. Then I have to get back to my quest."

The twins cheered and hopped on Twilight's back for a ride to the bakery. "Giddy-up!" they chorused.

✳ ✳ ✳

"Mrs. Cake, this rainbow chip…*mmmf*… delight is…*mmmf*…delicious," Twilight said with a full mouth. A dollop of pink icing made its way down her chin. Rarity would have been appalled at her bad mane-ers. "Excuse me," she said as she cleaned her face. "I don't mean to eat and run like this, but I really must be on my way."

"Of course, Princess," Mrs. Cake said, bowing quickly. She stood up and continued to pipe a tube of icing onto a strawberry layer cake, creating a beautiful border of plump roses in the process.

Twilight blushed with embarrassment. "You really don't have to call me that," Twilight replied. This *princess* business was tricky. Maybe she should put up a banner in the town square telling everypony to treat her as they normally would. "I'm just the same old Twilight, really."

She caught sight of her reflection in the shiny cake display case. Other than the new wings, she still looked the same. She wasn't even wearing her tiara. "In fact, I don't really know how to be a princess at all. That's what I'm doing today. I'm trying to ask some older ponies what it means to be a leader, but I don't want to ask Princess Celestia—that would be embarrassing—and when I tried

to go see Mayor Mare, she was busy and..."
Everything seemed to spill out at once.

Mrs. Cake furrowed her brow in motherly concern. "My goodness, that sounds like quite the sticky situation. Why don't you visit your big brother and Princess Cadance?"

Twilight brightened at the suggestion. What a great idea! Her BBBFF (Big Brother Best Friend Forever) Shining Armor and new Pegasister-in-law had much more royal experience than she did. Older siblings were practically made for giving guidance. "You're a genius! They are bound to have some royal advice!"

Carrot Cake popped his head in from the storeroom. "We're not out of royal icing! We have a whole carriage full back here, my dear!"

"No, Carrot," Mrs. Cake shouted back.

"Royal *advice*. For Twilight!" She shook her head and then sighed. "Stallions. They never listen."

Twilight chuckled as she made her way out the door. "In that case, maybe I'd better talk to Cadance and *not* Shining Armor." She was feeling much more confident now that she had a real plan. "Thanks for the terrific tips and treats, Mrs. Cake! Bye, Pumpkin! Bye, Pound!" And then the young monarch was off to the Crystal Empire to find out exactly what made a royal pony tick. Or at least talk.

Empire State of Mind

★ ★ ★

Twilight Sparkle didn't think it was possible, but the Crystal Empire looked even more beautiful than the last time she'd been there. The winding, cobble-gem streets and tall spires sparkled and glistened in the sunshine. Every facet of shining glass turned a different hue when the light danced on it. It had been a long journey, but it was well worth it to be back. As she entered through the front gates, Twilight felt a sense of overwhelming pride in her brother's new realm.

Everything appeared to be fully restored back to its former glory, partly thanks to her, of course, though she would never brag about it. The Crystal Empire had been through many dark days after the evil King Sombra tried to keep the source of the Empire's power—the Crystal Heart—hidden away. The Crystal Heart, charged by the power of the ponies' love, was the only object that was able to offer the Empire protection. Once it was stolen, the kingdom was overtaken by darkness.

Luckily, Princess Celestia had put Twilight to the test when she recruited her and her best friends to help. They came to the rescue, putting on the long-forgotten Crystal Faire while Twilight searched for the Empire's beloved Crystal Heart. When Twilight finally succeeded in recovering the precious, magical gemstone, not only did she pass her test, but balance was also restored to the stunning city.

As Twilight walked past a group of Crystal ponies, she smiled and waved. "Good afternoon, everypony!"

"Hey, Princess Twilight Sparkle!" they shouted in response. "Welcome back!"

A sparkling teal-colored pony with a light blue mane jumped up and down in excitement. The pony was named Glitter

Dance and reminded Twilight of her eternally energetic friend, Pinkie Pie. "We're going to the Crystal Lake today!" she exclaimed. "Come play with us!"

Twilight politely declined but was pleased by the invitation. The ponies were having tons of fun with one another, which was always a good sign. Every corner of the kingdom appeared to be filled with light and love. It was certainly the perfect place for Shining Armor and Princess Cadance to live and rule. Of course, having Cadance as their princess had likely contributed to the warm, fuzzy feelings of the Crystal pony population.

"Twily!" a handsome white stallion with a blue mane yelled from across the courtyard. Shining Armor hadn't seen his sister since her coronation. He galloped over and embraced her in a classic big-brother hug.

"How's my second-favorite princess?" He knocked her cheek lovingly with his hoof.

"Hey, now!" Twilight laughed. "I was around first!"

"Only kidding!" he said as Princess Cadance trotted over to join them. "You're *both* my favorite princesses."

"Cadance!" Twilight called out. "*Sunshine…sunshine…*" she started, looking to the elegant princess for acknowledgment.

"*Ladybugs awake!*" Cadance yelled in joyous response.

The two of them sang in unison as they hopped around and shook their tails at each other. "*Clap your hooves and do a little shake!*" It had been their secret tailshake since Twilight was just a little filly and Cadance was her foalsitter. It was still amusing after all these years, even though a couple of nearby ponies watched the scene in slight confusion. It was unusual to see their composed princess acting so silly.

"So what brings you to the Crystal Empire, little sis?" Shining Armor asked. "Isn't royal life great?" He beamed with pride and smiled wide. His little sister had come so far in her studies that she'd achieved princess status. It was very impressive, and he loved to tell other ponies all about her accomplishments. But ever since she was crowned, it was no secret to anypony. Twilight was famous all across Equestria now.

"Well...that's sort of why I'm here." Twilight dropped her eyes to the ground and scuffed a hoof around. "I'm not good at being a leader of other ponies. I don't know how to act! I don't feel anything like a princess, and it's just weird to have everypony

call me that. I don't feel very graceful....
Not like you, Cadance."

"Oh, Twilight!" said Shining Armor. "It isn't an easy transition. But you are doing great!"

Twilight knew he was trying to help, but she couldn't resist rolling her eyes a little bit. "Of course you would say that. You're my brother—you have to think so!"

"Chill out, Twily. Being royalty is a cinch! Right, Cadance?" He was clearly missing the point.

Cadance's face became serious. "No, Shining Armor. It's not as simple as that. I completely understand what she's going through." She turned to her fellow princess. "Maybe I can help you, Twilight."

She started by leading Twilight Sparkle down the street and through the city. Twilight was happy to follow.

CHAPTER 4

A Tail to Tell

★ ★ ★

It was a busy day in the Crystal Empire. The streets were bustling with Crystal ponies rushing home from the markets and shops, their packs filled with fresh apples and other luxuries.

"Good afternoon, Moondust!" Cadance

greeted an iridescent white pony with a sleek silver mane. She was selling baskets of Crystal berries (an Empire specialty) at a little stand near the fountain. "How are your foals doing?"

The pony beamed as she bowed to the two princesses. "They are wonderful! Would you like some fresh Crystal berries?" Moondust asked, and gave them each a small bunch. The sweet tartness exploded in Twilight's mouth as she devoured them. Twilight made a mental note to bring some back for the Cakes. The berries would definitely taste delicious in a pie.

"Thank you very much!" Twilight said as they walked away. How did Cadance do that—remember the names of a whole kingdom's residents? Twilight sometimes found it difficult to remember the names of just the entire Apple family. So far in the Empire, she'd met Topaz Twist, Citrine Star, Rosie Quartz, and now Moondust! Cadance's memory was impressive. Twilight wondered if she studied every night.

"I always try to remember everypony in the kingdom, because each one is special," Cadance explained as they walked. "We all play our part in making the kingdom a happy and fun place to live." Twilight sighed. Cadance definitely had a point, but all these new responsibilities were starting to add up. Maybe she could make flash cards with each pony's picture on it.

"You're such a great princess, Cadance," Twilight said. They approached a young Crystal pony couple, who smiled and bowed as the princesses passed them. "I wish I could be like you. I feel so lost."

"You know," Cadance offered, "I didn't always feel so confident."

"You didn't?" Twilight asked, trying to think of a time when Cadance had seemed as lost as she felt now.

"When I was found as a baby Pegasus, in a forest far, far away…" Cadance began the familiar tale. Twilight listened intently as Cadance recounted her path to becoming the great pony leader she was today.

Cadance told her how some Earth Ponies from a nearby village took her in as their own little filly. And as she grew up, the natural love and compassion she had for others filled everypony with warmth and the urge to protect her. Cadance was definitely special.

But all was not well for long.

An evil pony enchantress named Prismia lived alone nearby. She rarely came out of her cottage because she felt nothing but jealousy for the other ponies in the village— the way they loved and took care of one another. And yet, she had nopony who cared for her. Prismia always wore a powerful necklace, which she cared for more than anything else in the world, and it served to amplify the evil and jealousy within her own heart. When Prismia's bad feelings and the power of the necklace finally overtook her, she cast a spell on the villagers that leeched all the love from their homes. She hoped to capture some of that love for herself. Everypony was distraught and sad.

Cadance decided that she couldn't let that happen, so she went to see Prismia. Luckily, the enchantress's powerful necklace also amplified the power of Cadance's love, and she soon defeated Prismia with her incredible gift of compassion. Once Prismia changed her horrible ways, Cadance was surrounded by magical energy and transported to a strange place—a place that nopony except Princess Celestia had ever been! So when Celestia discovered special little Cadance in that mysterious location, her fate was sealed. The princess brought her back to Canterlot to raise her as her very own royal niece—the special and loving young Princess Cadance.

Princess Cadance's special talent had always been her amazing ability to spread love wherever she went—settling conflicts and bringing ponies of all kinds together. In her final exam at Celestia's school of magic, Cadance was even able to make two known rival pony families of Canterlot become best friends for life.

"So I spent a long time in Canterlot just resolving conflicts whenever I was needed and helping other ponies find love. I never really experienced it for myself." Cadance blushed a little and giggled. "Even though I *did* have a crush on your brother."

Twilight made a disgusted face. "Yuck."

"Everyone was telling me what a great princess I would be someday, but I just didn't feel like I knew what to do!" Cadance said. Twilight nodded in enthusiastic agreement. Now they were talking. "So I went to Princess Celestia for advice."

"And...?" Twilight asked, all ears.

"She asked me if I *felt* like a true leader." Cadance stopped walking and turned to her young companion. "I told her that no, sadly, I didn't."

"And…?" Twilight repeated again. She could hardly take the suspense!

Cadance continued, "She told me about an ancient spell that had the power to make anypony who was destined to lead become the pony they were meant to be."

Twilight smiled. She *knew* that there was an answer to all of this—and of course it was a spell!

True leadership was only an enchantment away.

✳ ✳ ✳

The two ponies soon found themselves standing in front of a giant crystal statue of Cadance. The sun shone through it, creating hundreds of tiny rainbows in the water flowing through the fountain. "Wow, they must… really love you a lot here, Cadance." Twilight cocked her head to the side. She could never imagine having a statue of herself. It was a bit much.

Cadance shook her head and shrugged. "Oh, I guess so!" she said, chuckling.

The famous, powerful Crystal Heart stood next to the statue, shining brilliantly with the magic of the Crystal ponies. Thankfully, it was safely displayed right where Twilight had last left it, rather than hidden away with some evil king. Rescuing the heart once had been difficult enough. She didn't want to have to do it again.

"So where can I find this leader spell, then? Can you teach it to me? Is it in one of the old spell books?" Twilight asked eagerly.

As soon as she learned the words from Cadance, she'd be on her way back to Ponyville. Then everything would be solved.

"Oh, no, Twilight." Cadance shook her head. "This spell isn't something that can just be learned. The Crystal Heart Spell can only be revealed when a future leader of Equestria understands what her biggest challenge in leadership will be. Only then will she know how to rule, in her heart."

Twilight furrowed her brow in confusion. What in Equestria was Cadance talking about? *Revealed*? Twilight was somehow supposed to get some random spell to appear out of thin air? This was going to be trickier than she'd expected.

"How in the hoof am I supposed to do that?!"

"I can help you with one clue, just as

Celestia did with me." Cadance's voice was gentle and reassuring. "Just think about the elements that make up a great kingdom, Twilight."

"The Elements of Harmony?" Twilight asked. It was the first thing that popped into her mind, so it probably was too obvious.

"Not exactly..." Cadance said. "What are the best things we have in Equestria?"

Twilight cocked her head to the side, completely baffled. Cadance thought it might be time for a different approach. So she began to recount her search for the spell in greater depth. Cadance warned Twilight, though, that the spell worked differently for everypony. It couldn't be repeated.

"Once I received the clue myself, I decided to start by asking my friends what they thought," Cadance remembered. "They had all sorts of crazy ideas about what they liked in a kingdom."

"Like what?" Twilight was soaking everything in like a sponge. This would all be useful in helping her find the Crystal Heart Spell.

"Well, my friend Buttercream said she thought every kingdom should have a chocolate fountain in the center. And another pony I knew, Sky Chariot, suggested a curfew time for all ponies to be home by." Cadance scrunched up her face in distaste. "I didn't really agree with any of them, but I used their ideas anyway."

Twilight nodded along as she listened to the story.

"But nothing happened!" Cadance said

dramatically. "The spell was nowhere to be found, and I was more lost than ever."

Twilight's eyes grew wide. "So how did you find it?"

"One day, I was sitting by the lake just outside Canterlot, reflecting on the situation," Cadance recalled. "I thought about how all I had ever done was listen to the suggestions or commands of other ponies."

"Like the way they would always ask you to help them fall in love?" Twilight asked.

"Yes, exactly! I never made any decisions for myself." Cadance stared out into the water of the crystal fountain. "As soon as I realized this, the spell appeared, shimmering in gold letters on the surface of the lake."

"Wow..." Twilight cooed, imagining the

pretty scene. Maybe she should go visit the Crystal Lake after all.

"As soon as I read the spell aloud, I instantly knew that my destiny was to lead other ponies with my strengths of True Love and Tolerance. But the only way to do it was by listening to my *own* heart as well."

A gift Horse

★ ★ ★

Cadance led Twilight through a massive wooden door and into a lush castle bedroom. It was decked out in rich, royal velvets of deep purple and gold. Hundreds of precious gems of every color adorned the bed frame and hung from the chandelier. The early-evening light shining through tall, gilded windowpanes was dazzling. It raked across the gray and silver stones of the walls and onto the lavish furnishings. With all the glitz, the castle quarters would have suited Rarity perfectly. The only thing about it that screamed "Twilight" was the fully stocked bookcase in the corner.

Twilight blinked her eyes in disbelief. "This room is all mine?"

"Well, not *all* yours!" Spike popped out from behind the purple drapes and did a little vaudeville dance. "Surprise!" Cadance laughed at the little dragon's antics.

"Spike!" Twilight exclaimed, and instantly felt guilty for leaving him behind earlier. "Sorry I left Ponyville in such a rush. You know how I get when I'm on a mission."

"Do I ever!" said Spike. "It's just lucky

you came back here when you did. I almost ate that entire bed frame while I was waiting for you." Spike's eyes grew large with longing as he looked around the room. Jewels and crystals were his favorite meal. It had taken a lot of self-control to keep from nibbling the furniture.

"Good thing you didn't." Twilight's eyes landed on a small, wrapped golden box with a bow on top. It was sitting in the center of the bed. "Spike, you didn't have to bring me a present. It's not even my birthday!"

"But I didn't...." Spike scratched his head. "I don't even know where that came from!"

"It's from me," Cadance said, nudging it toward Twilight with her muzzle. "Just a little gift from one princess to another." Cadance winked.

Twilight tore open the packaging. Inside was a beautiful necklace made of purple jewels. At the center was a large, prismatic gem in the shape of a heart. It had a special quality to it that Twilight had seen only one other place...around Cadance's neck!

"Cadance, is this your favorite necklace? From when we were growing up?" As a filly, Twilight had admired the necklace. It had always seemed to be extra special in some way that she couldn't quite put her hoof on.

Cadance smiled warmly. "Of course it is! I think it's time that a new princess wore it proudly."

"Oh, Cadance!" Twilight put the necklace on and spun around. Spike's eyes were glued to the adornment. Twilight admired herself in the mirror. "I'll take such good care of it! Thank you."

"Of course, my dear new sister," Cadance said as she made her way to the door. "I just want you to know one thing."

Twilight was still spinning around in front of the mirror, dreamy-eyed. "Yes?" she said, though it didn't seem like she was paying much attention.

"The rare gem in the middle has been enchanted with a powerful charm," Cadance explained. "As long as the pony wearing it is filled with the magic of love and positivity, the necklace will wrap her in warmth and protection."

"It sounds amazing!" Twilight said, looking down at the rare gem in awe. "Wait, is this the same necklace from the story? That Prismia wore?"

"It very well may be," said Cadance with a wink before she turned serious again. "But you must also remember that if the pony wearing it does *not* display those traits, it will only serve to magnify the negative thoughts and doubts within her!" cautioned Cadance. "Be careful, Twilight. Remember: If you stay true to your heart, the spell will soon reveal itself." And with that, Cadance was gone.

"Got it!" Twilight replied lazily, exhaustion from the long journey finally beginning to overtake her. She climbed into the cushy bed and nuzzled down into the covers. In the morning, she would begin to look for the elements of a perfect kingdom. "True to your heart…" she whispered before falling into a sweet, dreamless slumber. It was the sound sleep of a princess with a purpose.

* * *

She'd only been there a day, but Twilight Sparkle's Crystal Suite was already a mess. All the books from the shelf in the room were pulled out, littering the floor and bed. Some were open to pages filled with spells and history lessons; others lay closed in stacks. Spike sat on the window seat, gazing out at the panoramic view of the Crystal Empire and then looking closer with a telescope. He was trying to guess how many crystals were out there and also how yummy each one would taste.

"Where did Cadance say she started looking for the spell?" Twilight asked Spike, who hopped down and started restacking the books onto the shelf. It was almost like being back home in the cottage.

"I don't know!" Spike replied. "I was up here waiting for you, remember? I didn't hear her story."

Twilight wandered over to the box that held her gorgeous new necklace. It was sitting on a beautiful dresser with a mirror. As soon as she slipped on the necklace and looked in the mirror, she knew exactly what to do. "She asked her friends for their opinions—that's what Cadance did!" Twilight exclaimed. "Spike, take down a letter! No—make that *five* letters! I'm going to hold a secret spell summit with my best friends."

A meeting of the greatest minds in Ponyville was just what she needed to crack this case wide open.

CHAPTER 6

On a Scroll

★ ★ ★

Spike had been extra busy all day delivering the invitations for Twilight's emergency secret meeting. He'd visited Fluttershy's cottage first. She politely accepted and asked Spike if he wanted to come inside and play with her new fruit bat, Toby. "He's ever so shy, and I think he could use a new friend like you, Spike," she said in her tiny, gentle voice.

"Sorry, Fluttershy! I have all these scrolls to deliver for Twilight. Maybe Toby and I can 'hang out' later!" Spike chuckled at his own joke, but Fluttershy looked confused. "Get it? 'Hang out'? Because bats hang upside down?"

"Oh yes, of course. See you at the meeting!"

Next, he found Applejack working in the orchard at Sweet Apple Acres. She bucked her hind legs against a tree and a batch of juicy apples came tumbling down into a basket. "A meeting for Twilight?" Applejack looked relieved. "Phew! Nopony has seen her around for a few days! I was about to send out the Apple family search party."

"Did somepony say *party*?!" An excited

Pinkie Pie popped out from behind a tree. "Because my Party Watch just went off!" She held up her hoof to show Spike and Applejack a bright neon accessory. It looked like a watch, but instead of numbers it just had pictures of colorful balloons, streamers, and confetti with the word *party* spelled out twelve times. Little blinking lights rimmed the edge, and a honking noise was being emitted from a tiny speaker at the top.

"But where are all the numbers?" Applejack asked, confused.

"Who needs numbers?" Pinkie said, and shrugged.

"To see what time it is, silly!" Applejack threw her hooves in the air to illustrate her point.

"But it does tell the time! It's party time . . . all the time!" Pinkie shouted with glee. "Now who said the magic word, huh? Huh?!" She came up to Spike and looked him straight in the eye. "Was it you?"

"It's not a party, really... but here you go, Pinkie." Spike handed her a scroll. She quickly unfurled it and read the message. "A secret meeting party?! Oh goody, goody gumdrops! I have to go get ready!" And then Pinkie Pie bounced off toward her house.

"Thanks, Spike," Applejack said, shaking her head. "I guess you can count me and Pinkie in."

Rarity, on the other hand, was less thrilled about the invitation. She peered down at the scroll through her purple cat's-eye work glasses. "I'm in the middle of making a huge order of hornaments! Can this wait until later?" Rarity was always try-ing to finish some new garment or accessory for her Carousel Boutique. She was a very hard worker.

"Twilight said it was an emergency." Spike looked down at his feet. He didn't like to upset Rarity, because he really, really liked her. But she always responded to a few well-worded compliments. "Say, Rarity...have you done something special to your mane? It looks super-duper shiny today!"

"Well, actually, I did go to the spa this morning to have my hooves done and they gave me some new conditioner...." Rarity began to ramble. Five minutes later, Spike was still standing there. "...and then I said, 'Darling, if you must do my tail as well, just do it.' I knew it would be worth it!"

"Well, it looks great! Gotta run!" Spike quickly said before heading off down the road. He had spent quite a bit of time listening to chatter about the latest beauty treatments in Ponyville, and now he was running late. Luckily, he had only one stop left. Rainbow Dash was the last pony he had to invite to Twilight's secret meeting.

"Special delivery for one Miss Rainbow Dash!" Spike shouted halfheartedly at the clouds. He was ready to call it a day by the time he reached Ponyville Park. It was directly under Cloudsdale, so there was a good chance of finding the Pegasus there. "Rainbow Daaaash!" he called out impatiently. "I have a very important invitation to a very secret meeting at Twilight Sparkle's cottage!"

"Hold your ponies, Spike," Rainbow Dash said, swooping down from a cloud. "I'm comin'!"

Rainbow zoomed by a cloud that looked empty, but hidden inside was nosy Gilda the Griffon—and she had heard every word!

Suddenly, the "secret meeting" was not so secret.

* * *

"So what in tarnation is this all about, Twi?" Applejack asked as she bit into one of the apple fritters she'd brought for the meeting. All five of Twilight's best friends had shown up, even though surely they had other important things to do. Twilight knew she was lucky that they'd come to help her, no questions asked. It filled Twilight with a sense of pride and warmth that made her new necklace shine doubly bright.

Twilight cleared her throat and looked

at each of the ponies in the circle. "Thank you all for coming—" she began, and was immediately interrupted by Rarity.

"Is that divine necklace around your neck made of Cosmic Spectrum?" She stared at Twilight's new accessory with desire. "I have only seen pictures of it in books! My goodness, it's gorgeous! It almost looks like a mini version of the Crystal Heart." Rarity trotted over to get a closer look.

"Thanks! It was a present from Princess Cadance."

"You know what they say about Cosmic Spectrum…" Rarity added, turning to the other ponies. "When you wear it, you must remember—"

"Oh, totally. Yeah, I know all about it," Twilight said in order to keep the meeting moving. Twilight didn't want to listen to

Rarity talk about gemstones right now. The clock was ticking! Rarity shrugged, a little hurt. She trotted back to her spot and plopped down.

"*Anyway*, thank you all for coming on such short notice." Twilight looked around at each of her friends with genuine gratitude. "I've asked you here because I desperately need your help—"

"Ooooh! I know!" Pinkie Pie interrupted with a squeal. "You're planning an undercover jewel-heist mission and you want us all to join 'Sparkle's Six'?"

Twilight shook her head. "Not exactly, Pinkie."

Pinkie Pie was wearing a tan trench coat and a fedora hat in an attempt to disguise herself for the meeting. She had also brought along a drink she called "Secret Punch" as a refreshment, but she wouldn't reveal what the ingredients were, because it was a "super big secret." As a result, nopony wanted to drink it. "Or... you volunteered to plan this year's Hearth's Warming Eve pageant and you need us to help?!"

"Pinkie, it's still summertime," Rainbow Dash said, rolling her eyes. "I don't think that's it."

"Whatever it is, can we just get started?" Rarity whined. "I have lots of work to finish back at the boutique! Those hornaments are due in Mythica, Neigh York, by tomorrow morning and they aren't going to finish rhinestoning themselves. Do you have the time, Pinkie?" Rarity motioned toward Pinkie's Party Watch.

"Sure!" Pinkie said, and looked at her wrist. "It's 'party.'"

"Pardon me?" Rarity didn't quite comprehend. Applejack and Spike couldn't help but giggle, since they knew what was coming. "The time is party?"

"*It's party tiiiiime!*" Pinkie cheered, and did a skipping lap around the room. Everyone laughed except Rarity, who just looked annoyed.

"Okay, everyone! That's enough," Twilight said. "Down to business."

The ponies finally listened as Twilight recounted her trip to the Crystal Empire, sparing no details. She told them all about Cadance's journey to find the Crystal Heart Spell. Twilight explained that the only way she herself would find it was with the help of her friends. Just like Cadance.

"So I'll need you all to come up with some ideas for my future kingdom. If you don't, I'll never find the spell and I'll never learn to be a leader and I'll never be a great princess!" Twilight said in one breath. She had the tendency to exaggerate things.

"Calm down, Twilight," Fluttershy said, patting her on the back. "I'm sure that we can all figure this out together."

"Together?" Twilight asked hopefully. "You'll help me?"

The rest of the ponies nodded and held up their full cups of Secret Punch in a toast. "Together!"

CHAPTER 7

Brainstorming the Castle

★ ★ ★

The six ponies had been brainstorming for-ever, but Twilight somehow felt like she was even farther away from finding the spell than before. The conversation kept going in circles. They all seemed to have very different ideas about what they would do if they were in charge.

"There should be an official Cake Day!" Pinkie said, licking her lips. "Everypony in the kingdom just eats cake all day like a giant birthday party!"

"A royal guard made up of the fastest Pegasus ponies would be totally awesome," Rainbow Dash chimed in. "We could hold a race to find out who's the best." Then she pointed to herself. "Other than me, of course."

Twilight took note, but knew this was not the sort of information she was looking for. She sighed heavily. "Applejack? Rarity? Any thoughts?"

Applejack's eyes lit up. "Oooh! How about making everypony have dinner with their families every night like the Apple family does?" she said earnestly. "Strong families build a strong community."

"Okaaay," Twilight said, thinking of her own brother and parents and how far away they lived. It was a nice thought, but it wasn't a practical suggestion. Not everypony was lucky enough to live near their family like Applejack.

"I have an idea!" Fluttershy offered.

"You do?" Twilight replied, her ears perking up. Fluttershy was soft-spoken, but she could be very creative and surprising. "Tell me!"

"I was just thinking how great it would be if there were a place where all the baby animals could play together in safety, far from the scary creatures of the Everfree Forest. Like a nature reserve, but just for baby animals! That's what I would do." She stared dreamily out the window, imagining playing with all the adorable animals.

"Ummm…okay," Twilight said, and wrote down the idea.

Twilight was starting to rethink her plan. She needed real ideas about how a kingdom works, not silly ones about baby animals and cakes. "Rarity, any ideas? You've been awfully quiet over there."

"Well, sure. If you *actually* want my opinion now…" Rarity grumbled. Ever since she'd tried to warn Twilight about the necklace and was shut down, Rarity hadn't felt like saying a peep. "I would design a fashion line, just for the kingdom. Exclusive pieces made from extravagant fabrics so that everypony would look and feel their best!"

Pinkie Pie and Fluttershy nodded in excited agreement, but Twilight wasn't impressed. "Fashions, Rarity?" Twilight shook her head in defeat. "Come on, you guys! Think outside the box!"

"Well, sorry if my idea wasn't good enough for you, *Princess*," Rarity replied, and stuck her nose in the air. "I wish you luck in coming up with a better one." Then she trotted out of Twilight's cottage in a huff.

"Whoops," Twilight said, finally realizing she had hurt Rarity's feelings. "I didn't mean to make her feel bad. Guess I got a little carried away. Sorry, everypony. I guess that's enough for tonight."

Gilda's Got Game

★ ★ ★

Gilda the Griffon waited patiently outside Twilight's cottage until the last pony had left the secret summit. Pinkie Pie had hung around for ages giving her friend suggestions for different holidays to start and celebrations to throw.

"Thanks, Pinkie," Twilight said as she

walked her to the door. "I'll certainly consider making Gummy's birthday an official holiday." Gummy was Pinkie Pie's pet alligator.

"Great!!" Pinkie squealed. "He'll be so excited when I tell him the news!"

All of a sudden, a crazy noise started sounding from Pinkie's watch. "Gotta go, Twilight! I totally forgot about the house-warming party at Berry Punch's new place!" With that, Pinkie bounced off into the distance, singing a song. *"Oh, the bestest cottage is a warm one! A cottage that is filled with frieeends! So let's warm this house and fill it up with a party that never eeeends!"*

"Finally! I thought those ponies would never leave," Gilda said, swooping down from a cloud and landing softly in front of Twilight. "Productive meeting, Twilight?"

"Hey! How did you know about the meeting?" Twilight asked suspiciously. It was supposed to be a secret.

"I have my ways," Gilda said, pacing around Twilight. "And I listened to the whole thing. Didn't sound like your friends had *any* good ideas for your kingdom...."

"So what, Gilda?" Twilight sassed back. "You think you can do better?"

"I'm just trying to say that if *I* were a princess like you—I wouldn't be listening to anypony's suggestions. I would do whatever I wanted! Make my kingdom all about Gilda!" The griffon cackled and flew off into the clouds again to cause some mischief elsewhere.

Twilight brushed it off. Nopony in their right mind would take advice from Gilda, the notorious bully. Twilight still trusted her best friends the most. And why shouldn't she? They had proven themselves to be honest and loyal.

But then again, they didn't have years of magical study with Princess Celestia under their belts like Twilight did. And her friends had never even lived in Canterlot, so it was silly to expect them to know very much about being royal.

Twilight went back inside her cottage and looked into a large cerulean-colored chest. It was filled with her new gowns and jewels from the coronation. None of it seemed like hers. Twilight removed a tiara from its velvet case and placed it gently on her head. She looked in the mirror. The sparkling white diamonds and red rubies shone brilliantly. The tiara made her stand a little taller.

Maybe Gilda had a point. Maybe the

secret to leadership was listening to your own heart instead of everyone else's. Isn't that what Cadance had said?

If she was going to be a real princess, maybe she just needed to start acting like one.

✶ ✶ ✶

The aimless search for the Crystal Heart Spell was beginning to wear on Twilight, even though she was doing her best to try to act like a princess. She still didn't know where or how to look for it. It was making her crazy!

She even felt like she was hearing voices, which was never a good sign. For example, that morning in the Ponyville marketplace she'd asked Cheerilee which type of berries she should buy. Cheerilee had suggested the blackberries, but Twilight could've sworn she'd heard a voice coming from a stack of crates saying, "Who cares what *she* likes? What kind of berries do *you* want, Twilight?"

Later, when Twilight was looking after the Cutie Mark Crusaders—Apple Bloom, Scootaloo, and Sweetie Belle—she'd heard it again. They'd all been in Ponyville Park, deciding what afternoon activity to partake in. Twilight was getting frustrated because she really wanted to read the fillies a story from one of her favorite books, but all they wanted to do was jump rope. She was sitting by, watching them, when she heard the voice again. "Look at them!" it whispered. "You know what's best for them and they didn't even listen to you. You're the *princess*, for Celestia's sake!"

She'd looked around but hadn't seen any-pony who could have said it.

It was so odd. Ever since Gilda the Griffon planted the idea in her head that she shouldn't listen to her friends, Twilight had started to feel that everyone else's opinions were wrong. But was Gilda right?

Twilight decided to trot through the forest in hopes of clearing her head. The serene green trees and silence were usually comforting and helped her work out any problem she was having at the time.

She was only alone for a few moments, however, before a loud crash signaled the presence of another, familiar pink pony.

"There you are!" Pinkie Pie shouted through the trees. "I have been looking aaaall over for you! I want to show you my awesome plan for the new kingdom's holiday celebrations...and also play and hang out and eat cupcakes and all that super-duperiffic great stuff!"

"Thanks, Pinkie. But now isn't a good time," Twilight said calmly. "I'm sort of busy taking a walk." She motioned to the leafy path ahead of her.

"Okay! Will you be busy in ten minutes?" Pinkie asked, walking alongside her and smiling wide with excitement.

"Yes," Twilight replied. She was really starting to get frustrated now. She wanted be alone.

"Okay! What about in twenty minutes?!" Pinkie asked. She thought everything was a game.

"No! I'm busy now, I'm busy in ten minutes, and I'm busy in twenty minutes. I'm busy *all* of the minutes!" Twilight snapped. Her necklace began to dim, the colors churning. "Can't you see I don't have time to talk about your silly little parties?"

"What?" Pinkie Pie slumped to the ground, hurt. "Sorry to bother you, Twilight. I was just trying to help. I guess I'll leave you alone and go where somepony wants me."

"Finally!" Twilight sneered. "That's the best idea you've had yet!" As she trotted off into the distance, Pinkie began to wonder what was really going on with Twilight Sparkle.

This time, she didn't think it was something a party could solve.

CHAPTER 9

A Head in the Clouds

★ ★ ★

Twilight Sparkle was planning to ask Rainbow Dash if she'd seen Gilda the Griffon anywhere. Even though the two of them were no longer the best of friends, Rainbow always saw most of the comings and goings of the residents of Ponyville. There were great views of the whole town from up in the clouds, so she might know.

Maybe talking to the griffon again would shed some light on the situation. There had to be more to what she tried to tell Twilight the other night after she crashed the secret meeting. Or maybe not. But a princess should listen to everypony, Twilight told herself. Especially because she still hadn't thought of a way to find the spell.

Rainbow Dash was sitting on a cloud high in the sky. She appeared to be arguing with a large group of Pegasi. She didn't hear Twilight trying to call her from below. *Good thing I have wings now*, Twilight thought, taking off. She enjoyed the rush of cool air as she soared into the sky. It was fun to be an Alicorn!

"I have herded more clouds today than

all you slowpokes put together!" Rainbow Dash shouted at the other Pegasi. "My skills are second to nopony!"

"If you're so good, Rainbow Crash, why don't you help out the rest of us?" a big stallion named Hoops shouted back. His cutie mark was three basketballs.

"Rainbow!" Twilight called out, but Rainbow didn't notice.

"You asked for it!" Rainbow shot back at Hoops, and took off into a showy barrel roll. She gathered a nearby cloud, combined it with two others, and then jumped onto it. A heavy flood of rain poured out the bottom of the massive cloud like a waterfall.

"Just call me Commander Hurricane!" Rainbow yelled, grinning from ear to ear.

"Rainbow Dash!!" Twilight yelled a little louder. Why wasn't Rainbow listening? A princess was trying to speak to her! Twilight frowned. "Rainbow! Listen to me!"

Rainbow Dash finally noticed her friend hovering there, looking a little strange. "Oh, hey, Twilight! Are you here to talk about my awesome plans for the new royal guard?"

"No." Twilight rolled her eyes like answering Rainbow's question was really hard work. "Have you seen Gilda?" Rainbow cocked her head to the side. Twilight was acting really weird, and the colors on her necklace were swirling around.

"Are you okay?" Rainbow asked.

"Of course I am! Now, have you seen Gilda or not?"

"I think she's down by the farm with Trixie," Rainbow said. "The two of them have been spending a lot of time together lately. If you ask me, it smells like trouble. Mixing pranks and magic is a bad idea, right, Twilight?"

But Twilight Sparkle didn't hear the last part, because she was already off, flying toward Sweet Apple Acres. She didn't even say "thank you."

CHAPTER 10

Drinking the Lily Pad Slime

★ ★ ★

A good patch of leafy foliage was always ideal for spying. That was precisely the reason why Twilight Sparkle often found herself hiding behind tree trunks and peering through hedges while doing various sorts of field research.

Today, Twilight crouched low behind a

bush near the barn at Sweet Apple Acres. She had spent the last ten minutes watching as Gilda and Trixie rolled a barrel of fresh cider from the stacked-up stores and dumped it onto the grass. *Glug, glug, glug.* The cider spilled out quickly. Why anyone would waste the precious cider was beyond Twilight's understanding. Yet the two of them snickered as they began to fill the empty barrel with some gloopy green gunk that resembled the lily pad slime from Froggy Bottom Bog.

"These ponies will never know what hit 'em!" Gilda laughed triumphantly. "This might be one of my greatest pranks yet!"

Trixie joined in. "And once the unlucky ponies who get a cup of 'cider' from this barrel take a sip, I'll swoop in and perform a magnificent spell to save them from the horrible taste!" She cackled.

"Personally, I think it's funnier not to save them... but whatever you want, Trix!" Gilda said. "This partnership is really working out." The two of them high-fived.

"Hey!" Twilight shouted from the nearby bush. "You two!"

Gilda and Trixie scrambled to cover up the barrel, and both stepped in front of it to create a shield. They looked all around but didn't see anyone until Twilight climbed out from behind the bush. A couple of wayward twigs were still stuck in her mane.

"What are you, the undercover cider police?" Gilda sneered. "Do you take all your orders from Applejack now? Or are you finally giving some orders of your own, like a real royal pony, eh?"

Twilight puffed up. She was a little bit offended. "Well, if you *must* know, I couldn't care less what you do with that cider," Twilight said, even though she knew she would definitely tell Granny Smith which barrel was filled with slime later. "But I'm here because…because…I wanted to ask you about…" Twilight couldn't seem to find the words to ask Gilda the Griffon for help.

Trixie tapped her hoof on the grass impatiently. She was still wearing her purple magician's robe and pointy hat covered in stars. "The Great and Powerful Trixie doesn't have all day, Twilight!" She was clearly still a little bitter about the time Twilight accidentally revealed her to be a fraud in front of all of Ponyville. Trixie probably didn't feel so "Great and Powerful" after that.

"What were you talking about the other night at my cottage?" Twilight asked Gilda.

The griffon crossed her arms and

shrugged casually. "I was just saying that if *I* were a princess, nopony would be allowed to tell *me* what to do." Gilda put her claw on Twilight's shoulder and dug in a little too sharply. "What is it that *you* want to do, Twilight?"

"I want to..." Twilight hesitated. It was a little strange to be asking for Gilda's opinion on the matter. But she *was* right. Why was Twilight spending all this time and energy trying to listen to her friends in Ponyville, when she herself knew exactly where to find the answers—the one place she always felt completely at ease, no matter where in Equestria she was? "I want to go to the library! The Crystal Empire Library!"

Gilda nodded in satisfaction. "I'll admit— the library thing is a little weird. But the Crystal Empire sounds awesome! Right on,

Princess Twilight! You always know what's best."

A moment later, Twilight's jeweled necklace began to cloud and darken even more. The transformation was so brief and subtle that Twilight didn't even notice.

But there was definitely a new determination in her eyes. And it was a little scary.

All that Twilight could think about now was that huge library in the Crystal Empire. It held hundreds of old books! There was no way the spell wasn't hidden in the pages of one of them. She couldn't wait to dive into her studies and hide away with her books for as long as it took.

"Thanks for your help, guys," Twilight told Gilda and Trixie. "I have to go to the Crystal Empire right now!" Twilight spread her wings and took off into the air.

"That sounds so totally awesome! I'm coming, too," Gilda said, flying alongside her. "Is everything really made of crystals? What are the ponies like there?" Gilda began to imagine all the innocent victims whom she could play her pranks on. It was going to be so funny!

"Trixie will go with you, too!" Trixie exclaimed, trotting beneath them. She pictured a whole new city of ponies who had never seen her "Great and Powerful" magic act yet. It was going to be glorious!

The two lackeys followed as Twilight soared through the air, winding through

Ponyville and unaware of everything in her path. Fluttershy, who was leading a line of baby ducklings back to their mother at the pond, noticed Twilight approaching. "Oh, hi, Twilight!" she said very quietly. She smiled and waved. "I'm so glad you're here! I came up with some new ideas for the baby-animal sanctuary that I wanted to share with you...."

But Twilight didn't even see her and swooshed right past. She was going so fast that Fluttershy's pretty pink mane blew out from the gust of wind Twilight's wings created. Rarity watched the scene unfold in pure shock. Who was this pony and what had she done with their best friend, Twilight Sparkle? Twilight always stopped to talk with her friends. Then Rarity noticed that the Cosmic Spectrum gem on Twilight's necklace had lost some of its luster. This was a bad sign.

"Oh, Fluttershy!" Rarity said, trotting up to her. She was carrying a large sketchbook in her pack. It was full of new outfit designs she had been drawing all morning for Twilight's imaginary kingdom. Even though she'd been annoyed after the meeting, she still wanted to help her friend.

"Do you think she heard me?" Fluttershy squeaked sadly. "Twilight would never ignore somepony like that on purpose, right?"

But before Rarity could mention the necklace, Gilda the Griffon called out to them. "Twilight is a princess now, you guys! She's off to the Crystal Empire and doesn't need a bunch of silly Ponyville friends like you holding her back. She told me so herself. So leave her alone!" Then she took off into the sky after Twilight.

Rarity and Fluttershy exchanged a worried look. "We'd better go find Spike," Rarity said, looking to the sky. "He'll know what to do."

CHAPTER II

Rallying
the Hoofs

★ ★ ★

Golden Oak Library looked like it was occupied—the lights were on inside. But Rarity and Fluttershy had knocked on the door three times and got no answer. "Is any-dragon home?" Fluttershy whispered, her voice barely audible, as usual.

Rarity scoffed. "You're never going to get

his attention like that! Watch and learn, darling." She stood up straight and cleared her throat.

"Spiiiiike! Are you theeeeere?" Rarity trilled into one of the front windows. A split second later, Spike flung open the door. "Hi, Rarity!"

Fluttershy wasn't offended that Spike hadn't greeted her. Everypony knew Spike had a major crush on Rarity. At least it had gotten him to open the door. He was holding a large tub of ice cream and looked like he'd been crying.

"Are you okay?" Fluttershy asked.

"Twilight left me behind again!" Spike wailed. "She went back to the Crystal Empire and didn't even tell me! I had to hear it secondhand from Cranky Doodle Donkey. He said he was walking by Sweet Apple

Acres on his way home and heard her talking about the trip with Gilda and Trixie."

"Unfortunately, it's true," Rarity said, entering the cottage. "We saw her leave."

"No good-bye or anything," added Fluttershy. "Just whoosh! And gone."

"I think we can all agree that Twilight has not been herself today," Rarity said. Spike and Fluttershy nodded. "And I think that necklace is to blame!"

"Huh?" Spike and Fluttershy were equally confused.

"Last night I was trying to explain that even though Cosmic Spectrum is a beautiful gem, it can be very dangerous if it is exposed to too many negative feelings. It absorbs them and makes the pony wearing it feel worse!"

"Oh no!" said Fluttershy. "Poor Twilight."

"I knew it wasn't her fault!" Spike jumped up in the air. "We have to go save Twilight. Together?"

"Together!" shouted Rarity and Flutter-shy. They all nodded in agreement. Now all they had to do was find Rainbow Dash, Applejack, and Pinkie Pie and explain to them what had happened. The sooner they rallied the troops, the sooner they could hop on the Friendship Express to the Crystal Empire for a rescue mission.

CHAPTER 12

Crystal
Clear

★ ★ ★

"Look, I don't care what the two of you do—" Twilight snapped at Gilda and Trixie. "Just stay out of my way and don't make any trouble!"

Twilight was almost to the Crystal Empire Library when she ran straight into Shining

Armor. "Twily? I thought you went back to Ponyville!"

"I did, but now I'm back again!" Twilight said, shifting from hoof to hoof anxiously. She was itching to look through those books. She just knew the answer was in there somewhere.

"Great! You should come have lunch with me and Cadance in the castle," Shining Armor said.

"That's so nice, but I don't have time— maybe tomorrow. I have to go! Talk to you later!" Twilight said, cantering past him.

He watched in confusion as she ran off down the street and around the corner. Normally, she was excited to see him. It was very odd behavior, especially for Twilight....

Shining Armor took off toward the castle.

He had to find his wife, and he had to find her fast!

* * *

It was a familiar scene for Twilight, sitting in an accidental fort made up of large, glittery books. She hungrily flipped through the pages of one called *Ancient Spells of the Crystal Empire: Volume Four.* After the first three volumes, she had begun to feel discouraged, but she soldiered on. The Crystal Heart Spell just had to be in there somewhere!

"Twilight! Are you in here?" Princess Cadance called out, her voice echoing throughout the cavernous library. Shining Armor had come to her straightaway after seeing his sister act so bizarrely. Something wasn't right, and he knew Cadance could help.

"Yes, I'm in here," Twilight sighed loudly from inside her book fort. She didn't want to see Cadance right now. She felt embarrassed for not making any progress at all with the spell. Cadance peeked through a gap in the precarious towers of books.

"Oh dear, Twilight…" Cadance shook her head. "It's just as I suspected."

"What is?" Twilight whined. "Me being as big of a failure as I am? A pony with no leadership skills whatsoever?" Twilight hung her head in defeat. "Celestia should just go ahead and revoke my crown now."

"No, no, no. You're not a failure," Cadance said. She pointed her hoof at Twilight's neck. The Cosmic Spectrum wasn't shining at all anymore. "Look! You've gotten so down on yourself and those around you that the necklace is magnifying your negative feelings!"

The young princess looked down at the gem, stunned. "I didn't even notice that the necklace had changed...." Twilight suddenly thought of all her friends back in Ponyville. Rarity had tried to warn her about the gemstone, but Twilight had been so distracted trying to find the spell that she didn't even listen.

Actually, Twilight had dismissed all of their ideas. She suddenly thought of Pinkie Pie's cake day, Applejack's family dinner time, Rainbow Dash's Pegasus royal guard, Fluttershy's baby-animal sanctuary, and Rarity's kingdom fashions. The ideas didn't seem so bad now. Her friends were only trying to help her, like she'd asked them to.

And how did she thank them? By ignoring them and thinking only of herself.

"Oh, Cadance, I've been so horrible to my friends!" Twilight said, standing up. Several nearby books toppled over like a set of building blocks. "All I have been doing is thinking about what I want and not listening to anypony else's ideas!" The necklace began to glow dimly. "I have to go find my friends right now and apologize!"

Princess Cadance grinned as she watched Twilight gallop out of the library. She knew Twilight was on the right track again.

PFF to the Rescue

★ ★ ★

"Where do you think she'll be?" Applejack said as the five ponies and their baby-dragon companion made their way through the front gates of the Crystal Empire. The last time they'd all visited was during the Crystal Faire. Everything looked just as pretty and shiny as it had before.

Rarity sighed, satisfied by her sparkly surroundings. "Why am I not a Crystal pony?" she lamented, remembering how her coat had become temporarily glittery when they'd recovered the Crystal Heart. Unfortunately, the effects had worn off.

"What's that?!" said Pinkie Pie, pointing to a large crowd of Crystal ponies gathered near the fountain. "Whatever it is, it looks like fun! I'm gonna go see!"

All of a sudden, a bright flash of white illuminated the sky. *Pop!* A loud noise rang out. It came from the direction of the crowd. "Come on, everypony!" Applejack shouted, leading the way.

Applejack shoved her way to the front. A red-and-white-striped tent was set up. Massive posters hung on the sides, praising the talents of THE GREAT AND POWERFUL TRIXIE, MAGICIAN EXTRAORDINAIRE. Gilda the Griffon stood outside the tent on an old apple crate. "Step right up! Step right up, Crystal ponies!" Gilda shouted, "Get yer tickets now! Step right up to see Equestria's most talented Unicorn—the Great and Powerful Trixie! Only three bits each!"

A yellow pony with a golden mane handed Gilda her money and entered the tent. Pinkie Pie looked around excitedly. "Oooooh! Does anypony have three bits I can borrow?!" She jumped up and down.

"Don't they know it's a scam?" Rainbow Dash said in disbelief. "I can't believe this!"

Gilda continued on, unaware that the Ponyville crew was standing in the crowd.

"Trixie is so powerful that she once defeated an ursa major—all by herself!"

A couple more Crystal ponies paid Gilda and entered the tent.

"Hey, that's not true!" said Fluttershy. "It was Twilight who did that. Well, she took care of an ursa minor, anyway."

"I can't stand by and watch this anymore," Applejack said. She trotted to the front of the crowd and hopped up onto another crate. "Crystal ponies! Do not pay to see this show! This griffon and Unicorn are con-ponies who are trying to steal your bits!"

A low murmur broke out through the crowd.

"What are you doing here?!" Gilda spread her wings and screeched. "First you don't know how to take a hint when Princess Twilight wants to get rid of you! And now you are ruining our show? You five are the worst ponies in all of Equestria!"

Trixie peeked out of the tent to see what was going on. The Crystal ponies all watched the scene with their jaws open. This was more of a show than they'd bargained for!

"Nopony wants you guys here!" Gilda yelled. But she couldn't have been more wrong.

"That's not true!" A voice pierced through the crowd and interrupted the argument. "They are my best friends, and *I* want them here!" Twilight broke through the mass of Crystal ponies and trotted over to her friends.

"What are you guys doing here?" Twilight asked. She couldn't believe they had come all this way.

"We came to rescue you, silly!" Pinkie Pie said matter-of-factly.

"I told them all about the necklace," Rarity explained. "We knew that you weren't being yourself."

"The Twilight we know would never be mean to her friends!" Fluttershy said.

"Or ditch us for those two!" Rainbow Dash added, motioning to Gilda and Trixie. The two of them were now bickering over whether to continue on with the show.

"I'm so sorry, you guys! I thought that listening to my own heart meant choosing whatever things *I* wanted in the kingdom." Twilight smiled, and the necklace began to glow. "Now I know that a princess is not defined by the things she chooses for her kingdom. All that matters is how she treats other ponies, especially her friends." She leaned over and pulled them all into a group hug. "Princess or not—we are all equal ponies!" Twilight said.

"Oh my, Twilight!" Rarity squealed. "Look at your necklace!"

Sure enough, the gem began to glow brighter than ever before. The light was low and pulsating, like a true beating heart. Nearby, the Crystal Heart grew brighter as well. It was almost as if the two jewels were linked by some invisible force. The ponies watched in awe as a gigantic, glittery rainbow suddenly burst forth from the center of the Crystal Heart. It arched directly into Twilight's necklace!

"Ooooooh..." everypony watching the scene cooed.

"Hey, look at that!" Rainbow shouted. "There are words on the Crystal Heart!"

Twilight knew it right away. The Crystal Heart Spell had finally revealed itself to her. She trotted over and admired the words, which were lit up in shimmery gold. She took a deep breath and began to read them aloud:

"Friendship is the creed.
It has been from the start!
It's the only way to lead—
with your Crystal Heart!"

Twilight's coat sparkled as the spell took its effect on her. *Of course!* she thought as she read the words. Friendship had always been the answer to her problems. Why did she think it would be any different once she became a princess? Twilight looked around at the crowd of Crystal ponies cheering her on, her best friends standing next to her, and her brother and Cadance looking proud.

Twilight finally felt like a real princess.

"Happy Cake Day, everypony!" Pinkie Pie shouted with glee, skipping through the center of Ponyville. Since returning from the Crystal Empire, Twilight had started using all of her friends' suggestions as practice for being a real leader someday. It was working out perfectly. Everywhere Princess Twilight looked, pony families were enjoying the special Crystal berry cupcakes and pies together. "Happy Cake Day!" they said to one another happily.

The Cutie Mark Crusaders had even made a banner that read PONYVILLE CAKE DAY! and hung it across the front of the town hall. "Great idea, Princess Twilight!" Mr. Cake shouted from the treat cart. "These things are selling like hotcakes!"

"They are hotcakes, dear." Mrs. Cake laughed.

"Don't thank me!" Twilight said, walking over to where her friends sat on the grass, enjoying their own Crystal berry cakes. "Thank Pinkie Pie! She has the best ideas!"

Twilight took a small bite of her cupcake, careful not to let her tiara fall off her head. Wearing it still took some getting used to, but everypony in town really liked it when she did. "In fact, *all* my friends have the best ideas."

Rarity smiled and winked at her. "So do you, *Princess* Twilight. So do you!"

you're invited to read

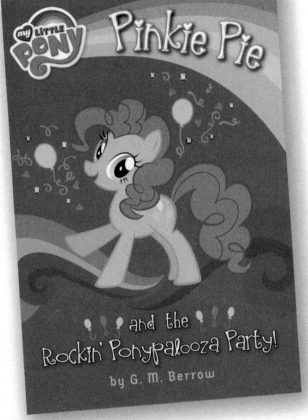

my LITTLE **PONY** Pinkie Pie

and the
Rockin' Ponypalooza Party!

by G. M. Berrow

Coming Soon!

Turn the page for a
special surprise from
Twilight Sparkle!

Dear reader,

I put together these bonus pages just for you! Have fun filling them out and sharing them with your friends!

Your friend,
Twilight Sparkle

THE WRITE STUFF

When Twilight came to live in Ponyville, the beautiful and wise Princess Celestia asked for letters about the lessons Twilight was learning as she studied the magic of friendship. Use the space below to write your own letter to Princess Celestia and tell her all about your friends!

Dear Princess Celestia,

My friends are named _____

_____.

Some fun activities we like to do

together are _____,

_____, and

_____.

Our favorite movie to watch together

is _____.

The best part about friendship is

_____!

I would also like to tell you that

_____

_____.

Your faithful student,

_____

MAKE YOUR MARK

When ponies discover what makes them special, they earn their unique cutie mark! What sorts of things do you like to do that make you feel special? What do your friends like to do? List them below and design your own cutie marks!

Name	Hobbies	Favorite Colors	Cutie Mark
Twilight Sparkle	Magic, reading, stargazing	Purple, pink	
Fluttershy	Caring for animals	Pink, yellow	
abby *(write your name here)*	animals cooking reading restlasting	bluck Magicng	
avery *(insert your friend's name)*	Reading	Pink red	
hannah *(insert your friend's name)*	cooking	greens periwinkle	

CAST A SPELL

As a student of magic, Twilight Sparkle has to learn lots of spells for different purposes. Unfortunately, there isn't a spell for everything. If you could recite a magic spell, what would it do? Write your own spell here.

Name of spell _____

Created by _____

Purpose _____

This spell is: *(circle one from each set)*

silly   fun   serious

easy   medium   difficult

It must be spoken in this type of voice: *(circle one)*

soft   regular   loud   extra loud

This spell must be repeated _____ times.

Write your spell here:

_____

_____

_____

_____

AT A LOSS FOR WORDS

Twilight has misplaced some of the words for her spell! Help her by finding and circling the words below.

P	R	I	N	C	E	S	S	P
S	C	N	Y	H	P	P	O	R
U	R	W	G	I	E	N	E	Q
T	Y	L	K	L	Y	A	A	H
N	S	E	L	V	D	L	R	S
C	T	W	I	L	I	G	H	T
A	A	L	H	L	P	Y	V	U
K	L	I	B	R	A	R	Y	D
E	F	T	I	A	R	A	Y	Y

TIARA CAKE TWILIGHT
SPIKE SPELL READ
PONYVILLE CRYSTAL PRINCESS
LIBRARY STUDY HEART

BOOK STARS

Twilight Sparkle loves to read so much that she lives in a library! Use the space below to list all the books you read. Each time you finish reading a book, give it a score of one star to four stars. Four stars mean you loved it!

Twilight Sparkle and the Crystal Heart Spell ★★★★

_____

_____

_____

_____

_____

_____

_____

_____

FRIENDLY ADVICE

When Twilight Sparkle is stuck on a tough problem, she likes to ask Princess Cadance for advice because her friend always has something wise to say. Whom do you go to for help? Why? Use the space below to talk about someone who offers help when you need it most. He or she might be a friend, a relative, or a teacher!

_____

_____

_____

_____

_____

_____

_____

_____

_____

A Daring Do Adventure

Studying is fun, but Twilight also loves to get lost in a good novel—especially stories about Daring Do, the fearless pony who goes on all sorts of exciting adventures through jungles and forbidden temples. Use these pages to write your own adventure starring Daring Do. Don't forget to include some daunting obstacles for Daring to overcome!

Once upon a time, Daring Do was…

_____

_____

_____

_____

_____

_____

_____

The End!

WEAR IT WELL

Twilight Sparkle is overjoyed when Princess Cadance gives her a beautiful heart necklace. What is your favorite thing to wear? What makes it so special? Describe it and draw a picture of it here!

My Jelly fish neklus.
why? Because I
got A realy bad
Jelly fish sting in
Jamaeia

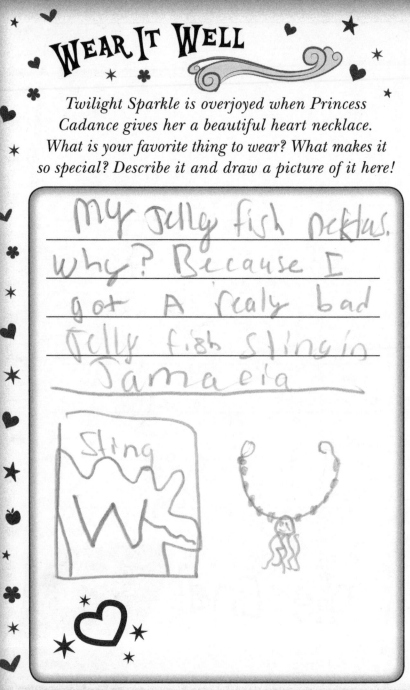

Sting
W

PONY SCRAMBLE

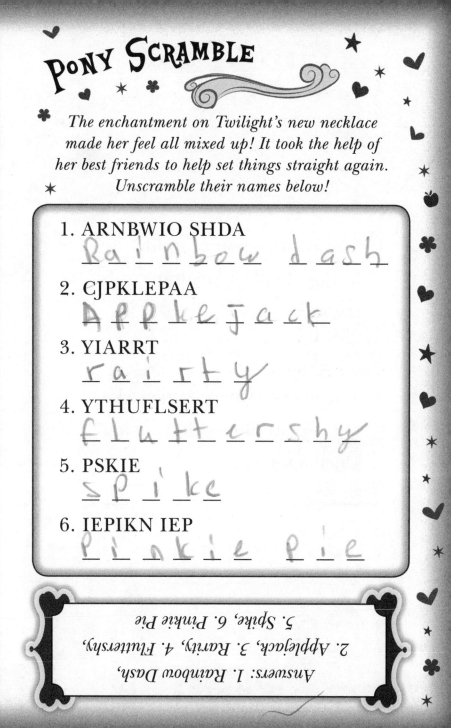

The enchantment on Twilight's new necklace made her feel all mixed up! It took the help of her best friends to help set things straight again. Unscramble their names below!

1. ARNBWIO SHDA

   Rainbow dash

2. CJPKLEPAA

   Applejack

3. YIARRT

   rairty

4. YTHUFLSERT

   Fluttershy

5. PSKIE

   Spike

6. IEPIKN IEP

   Pinkie pie

PONY TRIVIA TIME

Twilight has been living in Ponyville with her friends, but there are lots of other places in Equestria that she has visited. Use the clues provided to name some of them!

1. The Pegasus ponies reside in this cloud city high in the sky:

   Cloudsdale

   _____

2. The big city where Applejack once spent time with Aunt and Uncle Orange:

   _____

3. The stunning capital city of Equestria, where Princess Celestia resides:

_____

4. This sparkling empire is Shining Armor and Cadance's home:

_____

5. The dark and mysterious forest where Zecora the Zebra spends her days:

_____